Welcome to
Little Funnies

✔ KU-755-563

Little Funnies is a delightful collection of picture books made to put a giggle into storytime.

There are funny stories about a laughing lobster, a daring mouse, a teeny tiny woman, and lots more colourful characters!

Perfect for sharing, these rib-tickling tales will have your little ones coming back for more!

TEE HEE!

HA HA!

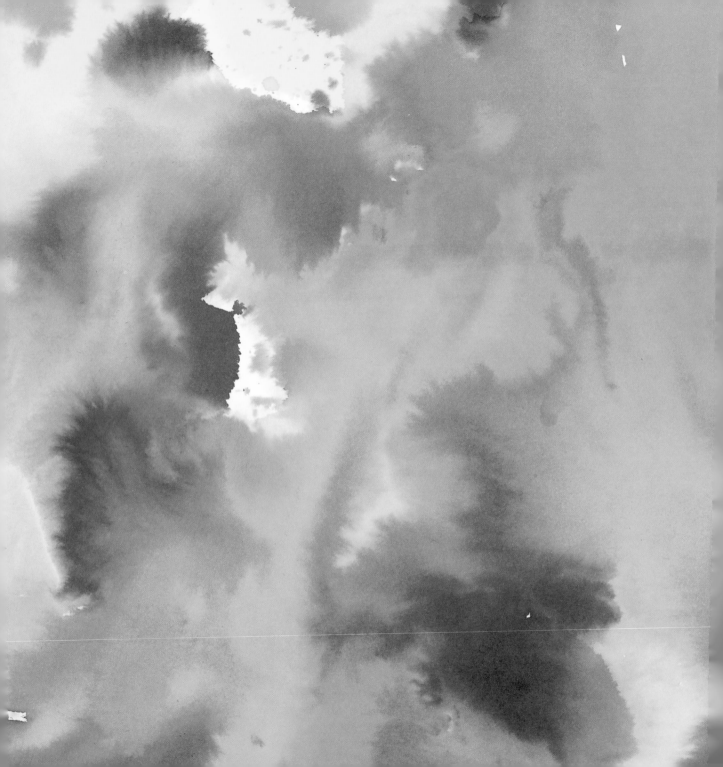

For David

First published 1996 by Walker Books Ltd
87 Vauxhall Walk, London SE11 5HJ

This edition published 2007

10 9 8 7 6 5 4 3 2 1

© 1996 Colin West

The moral rights of the illustrator
have been asserted.

This book has been typeset in Plantin.

Printed in China

All rights reserved

British Library Cataloguing in Publication Data:
a catalogue record for this book
is available from the British Library.

ISBN 978-1-4063-0792-4

www.walkerbooks.co.uk

"I DON'T CARE!" SAID THE BEAR

Colin West

WALKER BOOKS
AND SUBSIDIARIES
LONDON · BOSTON · SYDNEY · AUCKLAND

"There's a moose on the loose!"
said the teeny-weeny mouse.

"I don't care," said the bear,
with his nose in the air.

"There's a moose on the loose and a bad-tempered goose!" said the teeny-weeny mouse.

"I don't care," said the bear,
with his nose in the air.

"There's a moose on the loose
and a bad-tempered goose
and a pig who is big!"
said the teeny-weeny mouse.

"I don't care," said the bear,
with his nose in the air.

"There's a moose on the loose
and a bad-tempered goose
and a pig who is big
and a snake from a lake!"
said the teeny-weeny mouse.

"I don't care," said the bear,
with his nose in the air.

"There's a moose on the loose
and a bad-tempered goose
and a pig who is big
and a snake from a lake
and a wolf from the north!"
said the teeny-weeny mouse.

"I don't care!" said the bear,
with his nose in the air.

"There's a moose on the loose
   and a bad-tempered goose
   and a pig who is big
   and a snake from a lake
   and a wolf from the north
   and a teeny-weeny mouse!"
   said the teeny-weeny mouse.

"YIKES!" said the bear.
And he leapt in the air!

Then that great big
old bear ran off
back to his lair.